Pippin
Cleans Up

Pippin Cleans Up

Phylliss Adams
Eleanore Hartson
Mark Taylor

Illustrated by Gwen Connelly

MODERN CURRICULUM PRESS
CLEVELAND · TORONTO

ISBN 0-8136-5152-2 (Hardbound)
ISBN 0-8136-5652-4 (Paperback)   3   4   5   6   7   8   9   10   89   90   91   92

"Look, Herbie," said Pippin.
"People are cleaning things.
I'll see if I can clean, too."

5

A man was running a big machine.
The machine was cleaning the street.

Pippin watched the machine.
Then he sang.

> See the machine
> Sweep and beat.
> It makes the street
> Clean and neat.

Pippin jumped onto the machine.
He wanted to see how it worked.

8

All at once Pippin went up in the air.
He landed in a bucket of water.

A woman was washing a window.
Pippin sang to her.

Wash the window.
Make it shine.
Keep on going.
That looks fine.

Then Pippin looked in the window.
He saw a boy cleaning the floor.
Pippin sang to the boy.

Wash that floor
With your mop.
Clean and scrub.
Do not stop.

13

Pippin looked in another window.
"Just look at that," said Pippin.
"Those people are washing clothes.
I'll go and help."

15

Pippin helped a woman.
As he helped, he sang to her.

And a one and a two,
Now I'll help you.
And a three and a four,
Just watch me pour.

The woman did not want Pippin's help.
So she sang to Pippin.

And a one and a two,
I don't need you.
And a three and a four,
Now out the door.

The woman picked up Pippin and
put him out the door.

19

Just then Herbie's taxi went by.
Pippin jumped on top of the taxi.
Pippin sang as he rode along.

    Oh, what fun
    To take this ride!
    Herbie can't see me
    Because he's inside.

Herbie drove the taxi into a car wash.

And this time Pippin got washed!

Herbie found Pippin on top of
the taxi.
Pippin said, "Here I am.
I helped people clean things.
And I got clean, too."

Now Pippin was very tired.
So he jumped into Herbie's pocket.

Then Herbie looked at Pippin and sang.

Here in my pocket,
See who I keep.
Tired little Pippin,
Sound, sound asleep.

Pippin's Ride

If necessary, read these directions to the child:
Pippin had a ride on the big machine.
Trace with your finger the way Pippin went.

First, Pippin saw a man reading.

Next, Pippin went by a streetlight.

He rode by children swinging.

Then he passed an apple tree.

Pippin stopped at Herbie's taxi.

Cleanup Time

Look at the picture.
Find all the things that need cleaning.
Then find what could be used to clean each thing.

laundry soap

sponge

dustpan

broom

bar of soap

paper towels

dishwashing soap

mop

bucket of water

29

Pippin Cleans

This story tells how Pippin cleans.
Read each sentence in the story.
Then find the picture that goes with it.

First, Pippin picks up his clothes.

Then he washes the dishes.

Next, he dusts the chairs.

After that he mops the floor.

Last, he shines the windows.

In addition to many of the words used in **The Troll Family Stories** and **The Cora Cow Tales,** the following words appear in the story *Pippin Cleans Up*.

along	fine	land	sang
another	floor	machine	scrub
as	found	mop	shine
asleep	four		sound
beat	her	neat	street
because	Herbie	need	sweep
bucket	him	of	take
by	if	once	taxi
can't	I'll	onto	those
clean	inside	people	tired
clothes	into	pick	top
don't	just	Pippin	very
door	keep	pocket	wash
drove		pour	watch
		put	water
		rode	who
			window
			woman

About the Authors

Phylliss Adams, Eleanore Hartson, and Mark Taylor have a combined background that includes writing books for children and teachers, teaching at the elementary and university levels, and working in the areas of curriculum development, reading instruction and research, teacher training, parent education, and library and media services.

About the Illustrator

Gwen Connelly was born and raised in the Chicago area. After studying Fiber Art at the Penland School of Art in North Carolina and Fine Art at the University of Montana, she returned to Chicago to work as a designer, illustrator, and fine artist. Her talents are now concentrated on illustrating children's books.

Pippin came to life in the French carriage house that is Ms. Connelly's studio. The illustrator lives with her husband, daughter, and cat in Highland Park, Illinois.